THE WOODEN SWORD

A Jewish Folktale from Afghanistan

Ann Redisch Stampler

Illustrated by **Carol Liddiment**

Albert Whitman & Company
Chicago, Illinois

Library of Congress Cataloging-in-Publication Data

Stampler, Ann Redisch.
The wooden sword : a Jewish folktale from Afghanistan / by Ann Redisch Stampler ; illustrated by Carol Liddiment.
p. cm.
ISBN 978-0-8075-9201-4
[1. Folklore—Afghanistan. 2. Kings, queens, rulers, etc.—Folklore. 3. Jews—Folklore.] I. Liddiment, Carol, ill. II. Title.
PZ8.1.S7865Woo 2012   398.2089'9240581—dc23 2011015476

The design is by Carol Gildar.

For more information about Albert Whitman & Company,
please visit our web site at www.albertwhitman.com.

For my husband's parents, Marilyn Stampler and in memory of John Stampler.—A.S.

I would like to thank my editor, Abby Levine, for her dedication and the energy she devoted to getting every detail of this book just right; illustrator Carol Liddiment for bringing the story to life with warmth and color; my agent, Brenda Bowen, for all-around wonderfulness; Alexis O'Neil, Caroline Arnold, Sherill Kushner, Gretchen Woelfle, and Nina Kidd: critique group extraordinaire; Natalie Blitt, who led me to her favorite folktale; Diane Troderman, Harold Grinspoon, and Chris Barash at the PJ Library; Dr. Esther Juhasz, Tsila Zan-Bar Tzur, Ze-ev Yekutieli, and Shelly Rothschild, as well as the scholars mentioned in the author's note, for their help and unstinting generosity; and my family, for putting up with my obsession with Afghanistan.—A.S.

For my good friend Karen Napier . . . Things will turn out just as they should.—C.L.

One starry night in old Kabul, the good shah couldn't fall asleep.
He stretched and he yawned and he rolled out of bed.

Looking out toward the faint lights that glowed in the windows below, he
wondered if the people there were sad or happy, rich or poor, foolish or wise.

He climbed into his servant's clothes and slipped out of the palace so
he could wander through the streets and no one would know who he was.

The shah walked until he came to
the poorest section of the poorest street.
He stopped outside a home where he heard
laughter and singing. Inside he saw a
young man and his wife leaning together
over the nectar of sweet raisins by the
light of their two Sabbath lamps.

Asking himself what such poor people were so happy about, the shah knocked on their door.

"Come in and eat, weary traveler," the poor man said, "for we have plenty," although they had very little.

"Thank you," said the shah, feeling the contentment that filled the room. "What do you do that you are such a happy man?"

"I am a shoemaker. When I see a toe popping out of a slipper in the street, I mend that slipper then and there. With the *puli* I earn, I buy food for dinner."

"But what if one day you can't earn enough *puli?*" asked the shah.

"I don't worry about such things," replied the shoemaker. He cut up his last small apricot and gave his guest the biggest slice. "If one path is blocked, God leads me to another, and everything turns out just as it should."

The shah was greatly impressed, but he was very curious. He began to wonder just how strong the shoemaker's faith might be. Vowing he would let no harm befall the poor man, the shah decided he would test that faith.

The next morning, the shah sent messengers to every quarter of the city with a decree that no one could repair shoes in the street.

"This is terrible!" said the shoemaker's wife. "What will we do?"

"Don't worry," the shoemaker replied. "Life has thrown troubles in our path before, but no matter what comes, everything turns out just as it should."

With that, he walked through the city until he was parched. When he stopped for cool water, he noticed a water carrier filling up his bucket.

"Can a man earn his keep carrying water to sell?" the shoemaker asked.

"If he has strong hands, he can," replied the water carrier.

Quickly, the poor man filled a water pouch.
All day, he sold the water that he carted through
the winding streets. By evening, he had enough
puli to buy food for dinner.

When the last sliver of sun had disappeared from the sky, the shah said *Isha,* his evening prayer. Then he returned to find the poor man and his wife happy as ever.

"Come in, my friend," the poor man said. "Still in Kabul and still hungry, I see. Share our meal, for we have plenty," although they had less than before.

"I was thinking about you all day," the good shah said. "For when I heard that royal decree, I was afraid your God might have been . . . well . . . elsewhere."

"Oh, no," laughed the poor man. "He is always with me, and now I am a water carrier. It is a hard job, and I earn less than before, yet thankfully here I sit with all I need. So you see, things have turned out just as they should."

Perhaps that wasn't enough of a test, thought the shah. And in the morning, he decreed that no one could sell water in the streets.

"This is terrible!" said the poor man's wife. "What will we do?"

"Don't fret," her husband said. "Perhaps I cannot mend shoes or carry water, but I have faith that something new will come my way."

At that moment, a ragtag band of woodcutters passed by outside
the window! The poor man ran into the street.

"Can someone earn his keep gathering wood?" the poor man asked.

"If he has busy hands and a strong back, he can," replied a woodcutter.

With that, the poor man cleaned his axe. He chopped and gathered wood all day.

That evening, he sold the wood and used the *puli* he earned to buy rice for dinner.

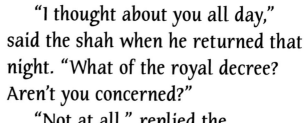

"I thought about you all day," said the shah when he returned that night. "What of the royal decree? Aren't you concerned?"

"Not at all," replied the shoemaker turned water carrier turned woodcutter. "I am blessed with a new job, and here I sit with all I need. Everything has turned out just as it should!"

Seeing that even his new test had not shaken the poor man's faith, the next day the shah proclaimed that all woodcutters would become members of his royal guard.

The poor man was proud to receive a silver sword and stand guard at the shah's palace, dressed in a fine uniform. At sunset, he asked the leader of the guard when he would be paid for his day's work.

"Your payday will come at the end of the month," said the leader.

"This is terrible! We will starve in a month!" said the poor man's wife when he came home with no *puli* and no hope of buying even one small apricot for dinner.

With that, the poor man went into the city and sold his silver sword for enough *puli* to eat for a month. While his wife cooked a hearty dinner, he used his axe to make a wooden sword. He thrust it deep into his scabbard, hoping nobody would notice.

That night, the shah heard the shoemaker turned water carrier turned woodcutter turned royal guard whistling a tune, happy as ever.

"I've been thinking about you all day," said the shah. "For when I heard you had become a royal guard, I wondered how you would buy food tonight."

The poor man told the shah how he had sold the silver sword and made a wooden one. "Things have turned out just as they should," he said.

The shah returned to the palace. He shook his head and wondered if there was any way to put that strong faith to the test.

The next day, he had the leader of the guard tell the poor man turned palace guard that in one short hour, someone had to execute a thief.

"Pull out your sword and cut off his head!" thundered the leader of the guard. "*You* are the royal executioner!"

"Cut off his head!" cried the poor man. "I have never cut off anybody's head, and I don't plan to start today!"

"You have no choice," the leader said. "It is the shah's command." The leader of the guard marched the poor man to a courtyard where a crowd was gathered.

"Excuse me," said the poor man quietly. "But would you mind if I prayed for a minute?"

"Pray all you like," the leader said. "It won't change anything."

The poor man closed his eyes and prayed until the leader boomed, "Off with his head! It's time!"

At that moment, the poor man knew exactly what to do.

"Please help me to do what is right," he prayed aloud. "If this man should be killed, may my sword have the sharpest blade in all Kabul! But if he should be spared, let my sword turn to wood."

Then he pulled out his wooden sword and held it high!

The crowd gasped, and even the leader took a step back, his eyes filled with wonder.

"Enough!" ordered the shah, stepping out of the crowd. "There will be no execution here today!" And he laughed, for there was no thief, and there had been no execution planned.

"You are the shah!" quaked the shoemaker, recognizing his nightly visitor.

"And you are a wise man," said the shah.
"With my prayer, I knew just what to do," the poor man
said simply.

With that, the good shah brought the poor man to his palace to serve as his royal adviser.

"But how can one poor shoemaker advise you?" asked the once-poor man.

"I have been thinking about you all day," said the good shah. "And when I have the advice of a wise shoemaker and a thankful water carrier, a blessed woodcutter, a humble royal guard, and an executioner who will not raise his sword when it is time for mercy, I have faith that everything will turn out just as it should."

Author's Note

The version of *The Wooden Sword* retold here belongs to the Jews who lived in Afghanistan for more than a thousand years through the mid-twentieth century. There are many other versions; I grew up with a mean-spirited European one in which the rich man is a bully and the poor man rather sour. So when I encountered the beautiful Afghani tale, with the good shah and the poor shoemaker bound by mutual respect, I was moved and inspired. For here the listener or reader—along with the story's characters—explores the value and resilience of an optimistic faith in the face of life's challenges, and how that faith enables even the humblest person to marshal his or her own resources and creativity to surmount obstacles large and small.

In my European tale, the poor man is clearly a Jew while the man testing his faith is not. In a version collected from an Afghani Jewish storyteller and published by Israeli folklorist Dov Noy (*Folktales of Israel,* Chicago: University of Chicago Press, 1963), however, the shoemaker's religion is not made explicit. Nevertheless, the intermingling of Jewish and Muslim neighbors in Afghanistan through the centuries, historical evidence that Jews worked in trusted positions for shahs, and my sense that the Afghani Jewish storytellers in the versions I've read identify strongly with the character of the shoemaker, allowed me to retain the religion of the shoemaker as he appeared in my childhood story.

Working with a folktale from outside my own culture was an adventure that impelled me to learn about the customs of the Afghani people, the clothes they wore, the role of women, what Jews might eat for their Sabbath meal, and which prayer a Muslim shah would say after dark.

I am deeply grateful to Shlomo Yekutieli, who grew up in Afghanistan and spent many hours describing Jewish life there, helping with every detail from the shape of Kiddush cups to the draping of turbans; to Professor Amir Hussein, who teaches and writes about Islam at Loyola Marymount University in Los Angeles and vetted the entire manuscript and preliminary drawings, answering endless questions to ensure that I hadn't made mistakes with respect to Muslim beliefs and culture; to Emanuel Yekutiel, who shared the fruits of his fascinating anthropological research within the Afghani Jewish community of Jerusalem; to Dr. Sara Koplik, for her knowledge of customs, social mores, and a history with dark and light moments; and finally to folklorist Professor Dan Ben-Amos of the University of Pennsylvania, who is always ready to share his extraordinary knowledge of folklore and its origins and to suggest resources, and who introduced me to another Afghani version of this story.